Christy, Katy, John
and the
TIME
MACHINE
Dancing with Running Deer

I0726558

ROBERT H. WELLINGTON III

Christy, Katy, John and the Time Machine: Dancing with Running Deer

Copyright © 2021 Robert H. Wellington III

Library of Congress Control Number   2021923660
Paperback   978-1-68547-039-5
Hardcover   978-1-68547-040-1
eBook   978-1-68547-041-8

Published 11/22/2021
Printed in the United States of America

FRISCO, TX 75034
United States
www.wa-publishing.com

Christy, Katy, John
and the
TIME MACHINE
Dancing with Running Deer

ROBERT H. WELLINGTON III

Hello, friends! My name is Kit Carson. I was named after the famous frontiersman from Taos, New Mexico, probably because of my feline curiosity and love of exploring. I am the head cat of this household, but my primary job is to keep an eye on Christy, Katy and John. It's a full time job, I can assure you. This is the story of how the kids and I discovered a magic time machine and the adventures which ensue. Follow my tail closely. We are about to embark on a fantastic adventure.

Christy, Katy, John and I live in a small but comfortable farm house near the Mississippi River in northern Iowa. It is a beautiful part of the country with tall bluffs by the river, and rolling hills cut by the mighty Mississippi over the millennia. Most of the hills are covered with hardwood forests, but as one moves further west, the forests give way to grass lands, and mile after mile of cultivated fields of corn, soy beans and all of the vegetables and grains that one can imagine. This was land with rich dark soil laid down over endless seasons, and today, is considered part of the breadbasket of America. It was an ideal place for a kid to grow up and explore. But most importantly, it was a great spot for an adventurous cat.

Every day after school, the kids would run outside to play and explore until their mom rang the big bell, known as Bong-Bong, telling them it was time for dinner. The bell, now on a stout pole and firmly cemented into the ground, at one time was mounted on an old railroad locomotive. Christy, Katy and John's dad had found it at the county flea market. He thought it would be perfect to signal the kids when it was time to come home from their explorations, which often took them far afield. The bell was solid brass, twelve inches across at the bottom and could be heard for miles. When John was little he called it Bong-Bong and it has been called Bong-Bong ever since.

Our favorite place to play and explore was a large hill and limestone bluff about a mile away. The hill was quite large, covered with countless giant oaks and other hardwoods. It had many secret ravines and rocky outcroppings to explore. We referred to it simply as Big Hill.

One day we were playing on Big Hill and I was following a small game trail in search of anything that moved, although it had to be smaller than me. The kids were also following the trail to see where it might lead. Although the path was well traveled and easily followed at the beginning, it soon led us down into a ravine and then to a tangle of wild grapevines, each vine about two to three inches in diameter. At the other side of the tangled vines was a limestone cliff about 25 feet in height, but the only way to get there, it seemed, was through a small opening in the vines leading to a dark tunnel. There was something about this trail. It had a certain mystery about it, compelling us to continue forward while also urging some caution. The girls were somewhat unsure about proceeding into the darkness, but for John and me, it was never an issue. I immediately jumped into the hole, hoping to find a small mouse or other treasure hidden in the thicket. John gave a sly smile to his sisters and followed me down the hole.

Once down amongst the tangle we found there was just enough sunlight filtering through to navigate our way slowly through the maze of growth toward the cliff.

Suddenly, we stopped dead in our tracks. Looking ahead in the shadows something was glowing. Not only was it glowing, but it was pulsating with a steady rhythm; it moved from a soft glow to an intense brightness and then back to a soft glow. John and I watched it for a few minutes wondering what it was. We were not in a big hurry to move closer, at least not until we had a better idea of what it was we were facing.

"John," we heard in a muffled tone. "John, are you alright? What did you find?"

It was Christy, who was beginning to worry about her brother's disappearance into the dark opening. She and Katy were about to climb down when John's happy face suddenly appeared in the opening.

"You are not going to believe what we found. Come quickly," John insisted. And with that his excited face disappeared into the shadows of the thicket.

After a quick look at each other, Christy and Katy gathered their courage, squeezed through the opening and quickly followed. There, just ahead of them, was the pulsating glow.

"What is that?" Christy said, catching her breath.

Katy, whose curiosity was overwhelming her better judgement, responded, "There is only one way to find out," and she crawled ahead toward the mysterious light. "It's a cave," she said excitedly. "There is a cave behind this boulder.

"Sweet," shouted John.

Indeed, there was a cave. Of course, if they understood cat language I would have already told them so. But, alas, it is a cat's fate to play the silent hero. They hadn't seen the cave because it was perfectly hidden in the shadows. Cautiously, they moved forward to see what Katy had discovered.

"Look, " said John. "Above the door."

There above the door, partially hidden by moss and lichen, was what appeared to be a petroglyph, an ancient drawing left behind by an ancient traveler.

"What is it, I wonder," Christy whispered as she removed some of the moss to see it more clearly. "It looks like an eight on its side, like an infinity symbol. We were just talking about the concept of infinity in school last week. But why is it here."

With our curiosity on high alert, we moved deeper into the cave and closer to the light. The cave opened up into a large room. On the walls were more symbols, just like the one over the door. There were others which we did not recognize, reminding the kids of some ancient alphabet.

They were now very close to the light. Rounding a bend in the cave they saw it. It's pulsating light lit the whole room. It was some sort of machine or vehicle. It had a distinctive geometric shape, about the size of a medium sized car.

"It's a perfect dodecahedron," exclaimed Christy. " We studied it and other geometrical shapes in school last year." The kids stared at it for a long while. What was it?

John, always the adventurous one, took a few cautious steps closer to the strange object. As he got closer, it glowed brighter and steadier.

"Careful," said Katy.

John slowly backed away. As he did so, it began to pulsate again. Noticing the pattern, John carefully approached whatever it was, and again it began to glow brighter and steadier. Christy and Katy followed their brother. When all were a few feet from the craft, a door suddenly opened.

Woah! What was that? They quickly took a few steps backward. At about six to ten feet of distance the door closed and the machine began to pulsate with the same steady rhythm as before.

"Do that again, John," Christy said, and he took several steps towards the craft. As he did the door opened and the craft glowed brightly. Seeing my chance I quickly jumped into the craft when no one noticed.

"Look at the cave wall behind the craft," she said.

The additional light had revealed hundreds of pictures or petroglyphs which couldn't be seen before.

The pictures were organized into groupings of a dozen or so. Each group seemed to tell its own story. One group showed what appeared to be dinosaurs, and another had wooly mammoths and saber tooth tigers. A larger grouping showed teepees and an Indian village with people riding ponies, shooting arrows or throwing spears.

"This is amazing," John whispered as if someone other than his two sisters and I were listening.

At the end of each drawing was a picture matching the craft, and what appeared to be a set of controls and dials with certain buttons highlighted or darker than others, as if they had been pushed and were part of an instrument console.

The kids moved close enough to the craft so they could see inside. They all gasped as Katy exclaimed, "They all match. The controls in the pictures on the wall of the cave match those in the craft."

"It's like each group of pictures relates to a different trip back in time," Christy said. There was a long silence as the kids pondered what they had just discovered.

"A TIME MACHINE," they all shouted simultaneously. "It's a time machine."

The kids were besides themselves with excitement. I, of course, remained calm. I'm a cat and I never show excitement…well, except for my tail which has a mind of its own, and too often gives me away.

"Do you think the highlighted buttons are controls which direct the craft to the particular time period and location shown by the glyphs?", said Christy.

"There's only one way to find out," John said excitedly. He jumped into the open door of the time machine and yelled to his sisters, "Let's go!"

"Wait a moment, John," Christy quickly interjected hoping to slow down her impulsive sibling. "We don't know for sure what this thing is, how it works or exactly what it does. What if it sweeps us on an adventure and we can't return?"

Christy, being the oldest took special pride in looking after her sister and brother and was not going to take an unnecessary chance.

"I think we need to take a closer look. Maybe something inside will give us a clue as to how this machine operates," said Katy, as she quickly climbed aboard.

" Ok, ok," said Christy. "We can look around, but don't touch anything."

With that, she also climbed aboard. In truth, she was more than a little curious herself. Inside there were three permanent seats and what appeared to be a fourth jump seat which folded up when not in use. I, of course, had already claimed the jump seat and had a perfect view of all that was going on.

"Look," Katy said. "Kitty C (which along with KC was her nickname for me) has already found a seat," as she gave me a scratch under the chin. I love it when she does that.

There was a large screen in front of the three permanent seats and just below it a panel with a few dozen buttons and two dials. One of the dials had today's date and time, right down to a hundredth of a second.

"Interesting," said Christy as she turned her attention to the second dial. This dial was similar to the first, but not set to any specific time. A wheel like device immediately next to the second dial seemed to adjust it. *Could this set the time for the period a traveler wanted to visit, she thought to herself?* Hmmm.

"Hello Christy, Katy and John. I have been expecting you," said a voice which appeared to come from the control panel.

"WHAT! Who said that?" the kids said in unison as they moved closer to the door in case they needed to make a quick escape.

"Please don't be alarmed," the voice said. "I am XJ. I am the computer that runs this ship. I will be your guide. I have guided many children on many adventures throughout time."

"How did you know our names," asked Christy, "and why do you call this a ship and what do you mean by adventures in time?"

"Hold on. Hold on now, all your questions will be answered, but one at a time or you'll fry my circuits," said XJ with a voice that was clearly amused at the kids enthusiasm.

"For several years I have watched you play on these hills. I am always watching, looking for kids with a loving heart to guide on adventures in time." XJ paused for a moment and then continued. " Only certain children are invited to travel with me, for only certain children can be trusted to obey the 'Time Travelers Code.'"

"The 'Time Travelers Code', said John. "What is the 'Time Travelers Code'?"

"The Code is about the experiences that time travel affords, and the living reality belonging to each time line or period. A visitor to another time period is allowed to observe the reality of that time, if you will, but must never interfere in a way that will change that reality or impact it in a negative way. That is why I observed you for a long time before I led you to this cave and let you see me. At all other times, I remain cloaked so that only those I choose can see me, and if they wish to, travel with me."

There was a long silence as the kids pondered what XJ had just said. Were they dreaming? This was a lot to take in. Time travel, a magic time machine, the 'Time Traveler's Code', being chosen by XJ; their heads were spinning.

"So, where do you want to go first?" XJ asked, breaking the tension of the silence.

Without hesitation John jumped in. "I want to see the Indians who lived here before we did. I want to see them in their native state, before the arrival of the European settlers."

"Yes, that would be wonderful," Christy and Katy quickly interjected, and I must say the idea sounded great to me also. Before they realized the ramifications of what they had just asked, XJ said, "So be it."

Certain buttons, similar to those on the cave walls, lit up and the second dial set itself to 1700. The time machine began to hum in a low tone while pulsating with light. The screen in front of them began to show scenes of Big Hill with each season flashing by, only in reverse order, summer, spring, winter and fall. Over and over the seasons flashed by at an ever increasing rate, and then suddenly it stopped.

"We're here," said XJ. I have taken you to the summer of 1700. When you go outside you will find yourself on Big Hill several hundred years in the past. I felt that on your first trip you would be more comfortable in your own back yard, so to speak. For if you look from Big Hill north you will see the valley where your family will build their farm house approximately 300 years in the future."

XJ paused to let things sink in and then continued, "The Indians who live here are primarily from the Sacs, Fox and Iowa Tribes, but you might also meet new friends from the Miami, Ottawa and Sioux tribes. Remember that the Indians do not refer to themselves as Indians. They are simply 'The People' or sometimes the 'People of the Snow'. In the Iowan language, it is Baxoje, pronounced 'Bah ko je.'

"Indian" is a name given to them by the early European explorers, who originally were looking for a trade route from Europe to India and Asia, but ran into North and South America first, as they sailed their ships westward from Europe.

The local Indians plant some crops like maize, but also subsist through hunting and fishing. Go and explore, but remember the Code and be back tomorrow around noon."

"Tomorrow at noon," said Christy. "Mom and dad will be worried sick."

"Not to worry, dear friends," XJ said quickly to put their concerns to rest. "I will have you back to Big Hill within an hour and a half from when you left. Generally a day of time traveling will be reflected as an hour passing back at your home. But remember, I am a time machine and can take you back to any time you wish."

XJ continued, "On this trip, you will be back in time to hear Bong-Bong call you for supper. Here, take this crystal with you. You will discover that It has many uses. It will begin to glow when it is time to return. It also will help you find me since I will be cloaked and hidden from all but you, so as not to impact this time period."

"Oh," continued XJ. " You may want to start your adventure by the river."

With that bit of advice fresh on their minds, the kids climbed down from the Time Machine, followed closely by me of course, and headed east toward the mighty Mississippi river. After a few steps they turned to look for the Time Machine, but it was nowhere to be seen, perfectly cloaked and invisible, just as XJ said it would be.

Christy carefully put the crystal that XJ had given them in her back pack. Christy always brought her backpack on their adventures. Among the various necessities, she carried an extra water bottle, Band-Aids and a small flash light. She could never be sure when her brother and sister might need her help.

I wonder what else this crystal does, Christy thought to herself, as she carefully zipped it into an inside pocket.

As they stepped out of the cave and into the sunlight, they immediately noticed that the tangle of grape vines was not there. In its place were a small grove of pine trees and a meadow of flowing grass, which in the wind waved like an undulating ocean. They looked north to where their farm house would be built in a few hundred years and there in the valley was a village with several teepees, bark lodges and a long house. There was smoke curling up from several fires and movement, as people went about their daily routine.

Looking eastward, they could see the mighty Mississippi and the familiar bluffs carved along its banks.

"Which way," said John.

"Well, XJ suggested we start down by the river," said Christy. "It's only a mile or two, so let's start there."

They all agreed and were on their way. They were somewhat amazed as they followed a well-worn path which 300 years later would be a paved road through the hills to the river. It was the best way through the hills and bluffs, so its location made perfect sense, but it was an interesting revelation nonetheless.

Everything was so pristine. Wild life was abundant and dozens of birds serenaded the kids with a symphony of sounds as they walked.

"I don't ever remember so many song birds," said Katy.

Even the small streams and creeks which flowed to the river were clear and clean, inviting you to drink directly from them. In fact, I took a moment and did just that. A cat can get thirsty chaperoning his kids.

Coming over the last hill, we saw it. The Mighty River. What a sight it was. The Mississippi was about a mile wide at this point and we could see a canoe traveling down the far side as well as the occasional fisherman with his net and fish traps.

Closer to the near shore, we saw a young Indian boy fishing with a net while standing in his canoe. He was intently searching the turbulent waters for any sign of movement.

Christy, Katy and John had played by the river frequently in the past, but they never ceased to be amazed by the powerful flow of this mighty river and its many currents and whirlpools as it makes its way to the Gulf of Mexico. When out in a small boat on the river, it was necessary to constantly be aware of the currents which were often impacted unpredictably by sand bars and various underwater formations.As we approached the river bank, our attention was again drawn to the young fisherman. He was dressed in a loin cloth and had deer skin leggings. His black hair was tied in a pony tail with a small feather attached. He was bare skinned from the waste up and had dark reddish skin from a life outdoors. He looked just like some of the pictures the kids had studied in their history class related to the woodland Indians.

"That's so awesome," John whispered. "A real Indian."

The young fisherman skillfully searched the water with net raised, while standing in his canoe which floated with the considerable current. He was quite skilled and already had caught one or two bass which lay in the bow of his canoe, but Katy thought he was getting dangerously close to a large whirlpool and began to worry. He seemed to be preoccupied with fishing and unaware of the approaching danger. Unable to control her protective instincts, Katy ran to the shore to warn him.

"Watch out," Katy yelled as the whirlpool was now only a few feet from the canoe.

Surprised to hear a strange voice, the boy looked to the shore to see who had yelled. When he saw Christy, Katy, John and me, he froze in amazement. Who were these strangers with light skin and hair and dressed in unusual clothes. He thought he was seeing spirits and couldn't take his eyes off these strange visitors. With his mind focused on the kids, he was totally surprised as his canoe hit the whirlpool and was violently spun in a counter-clockwise direction. Losing his balance at the sudden movement, he stepped on the side of the canoe and it capsized. Rising quickly to the surface the boy grabbed his canoe with one hand and attempted to swim it to shore with the other. The swift current had other ideas, however, and he made little progress as he was swept down river.

"He needs our help," John yelled, and the three kids ran along the shore trying to keep up with the canoe being swept downstream while at the same time looking for a branch or vine or something to throw to the boy to pull him to shore. The shoreline was covered with bushes and other growth which slowed their progress considerably, but with some effort they caught up to the canoe and the boy as they were being pulled downstream.

Looking around, John saw a long, thin but sturdy pole, perhaps a teepee pole left behind. That will be perfect, John thought. He sprinted ahead grabbed the pole and then ran along the shore to catch up with the canoe which was moving downstream at a brisk pace. Up ahead, the kids saw a spot where a sandbar reached part way into the river. It was just in front of the Indian boy. John ran onto the sand bar and reached the pole out into the river for the Indian boy to grab.

"Grab the branch," John yelled.

Not understanding a word that John was saying, but well aware that John was trying to help, he grabbed the branch. He held the branch with one hand and held onto the canoe with the other. The weight of the boy and canoe on the pole, compounded by poor footing in the sand, was pulling John into the river. In the nick of time the girls arrived. Christy grabbed onto John and Katy grabbed onto Christy. All dug in their feet and pulled with all their strength. Together they had just enough leverage to slowly pull the boy and canoe to shore, where he could get a foothold and climb out. It took all four of them working in unison to pull the canoe up onto the shore and away from the flowing water.

Exhausted, but proud of their joint effort, all four kids smiled at each other. I too was quite proud of them, having observed everything from the safety of a nearby tree. Once they all caught their breath, the Indian boy tried to communicate in his native language, but the kids didn't understand. The boy tried again, this time using sign language combined with his native language, but still they didn't understand.

Interestingly, every time the boy spoke, a voice crackled like a radio from inside Christy's backpack. She opened the backpack to see what was making the noise. Unzipping the inside pocket she pulled out the crystal XJ had given them.

"Oh my goodness," Christy exclaimed. "It's the crystal."

It seemed to be translating. Hmmm, thought Christy. I wonder what other surprises you are hiding from us,"

With that the Indian boy said, "Thank you my friends," and all understood what he was saying even though it was in his native language.

"You are most welcome," said Christy. "But I fear our warning you about the whirlpool may have actually contributed to the mishap."

The Indian boy responded, "Not at all, although it was somewhat of a surprise to see the three of you and your furry friend standing on the shore."

Furry friend, I muttered in feline, to myself. Clearly, he didn't know that my name was Kit Carson.

"I am Running Deer. Who are you and where do you come from?"

The kids introduced themselves, and me, and thanks to the crystal everyone understood everything that was being said. I wondered if the crystal could translate cat language, but try as I might, "Meow" was always translated as "Meow." They all sat down and began to have a long discussion.

"We are travelers from another place, said Christy, thinking it best not to mention anything about time, at least for now. "We would like to know more about you and your people," Christy quickly interjected, to change the subject.

"You must come to my village then," said Running Deer. "You rescued me from the current of Big River and therefor are a friend for life. You will be very welcome among my people."

They talked on into the afternoon, sharing stories about their lives. The kids noticed that Running Deer always referred to his tribe or village as "the People" and that they were stewards of the land, living off it while giving back in a balanced and conscious way.

Running Deer looked up into the sky. "The sun moves west," he said. "Come, I will introduce you to my people. You are in luck. Tonight the moon will be full and we will have a Grand Council to commune with the Great Spirit, Wauconda. Come."

With that, Running Deer, pulled his canoe further onto the shore and headed up the path past Big Hill and then on to his village. He moved along the path at a brisk pace, almost running. Christy, Katy and John soon realized why the People had named him Running Deer.

Along their way they saw hunting parties bringing their game back to the village. One hunter had just shot a deer and was kneeling next to it praying. The kids watched closely as they passed. They were struck by the solemnity and respectful gratitude which the hunter showed towards his quarry.

As they entered the village they observed people preparing food, mending clothes, chipping or knapping flint for arrowheads, repairing teepees and the bark siding of the huts and long house. No one sat idly. All were busy contributing to the needs of the village. They were so busy that they didn't notice the strange visitors with Running Deer until we were within the village limits. This didn't last long, however, and before the kids had taken ten more steps a large crowd had moved around them to get a closer look. Some reached out to touch them. Others let out whoops and hollers which soon alerted the entire village. I stayed in the shadows since there were a few dogs patrolling the village and I didn't want to risk an unexpected encounter, where I might have to assert my authority over the canines.

"Just keep walking," Running Deer reassured his guests. "They are only curious. Except for some of the Elders, few of us have seen people like you.

With their hearts beating a little faster, Christy, Katy and John continued to walk closely behind Running Deer, followed by their entourage of the People. He was heading towards a large bark long-house about twenty yards ahead, which he told us was simply known as Long House. Looking around as they made their way through the crowd, they couldn't help but notice that the village was preparing for some sort of celebration. Logs for a bon fire were being carefully laid within a large circular area outlined by elongated rocks about a foot to a foot and a half in length. The circular area was thirty to forty yards in diameter.

"This is the Council Ring where we will hold Grand Council tonight. Many will come from all the nearby villages," Running Deer explained.

He continued, "The Elders are in the Long House preparing. Wait here while I tell them about you. The people know that you are my friends and therefor honored guests, so feel free to move about the village. I will be back shortly," and he ducked into the Long House and disappeared.

The people of the village moved closer to the kids, greatly intrigued by their light colored skin and hair, not to mention their shorts, tennis shoes and tee shirts. Christy's backpack was of considerable interest, as was John's Iowa Hawkeye Football jersey. In their native language they buzzed endlessly about Running Deer's strange new friends.

Thanks to XJ's crystal, the kids understood everything that was being said. They stood there smiling with admiration and wonder for their new hosts. Despite this amazing experience, they were more than a little relieved when Running Deer reemerged from the Long House and invited them in. He smiled at his people and with sign language asked them to move back and make a way for his guests to enter the Long House.

I quickly jumped onto the roof of the Long House, feeling that this would give me the best view and perspective of the events taking place in the village, not to mention the safety it afforded me from the village dogs.

Inside the Long House, the Chief and Elders were sitting in a large circle around a neat fire with smoke curling up through a hole in the roof.

One of the Elders spoke, "Come in, friends. Join us. Sit down and let us share together." He had a large headdress with many feathers, each signifying an important event in the Chief's life.

The kids and Running Deer each sat cross legged at a spot around the fire. Before another word was said, the Chief took a burning piece of tinder from the fire and lit a beautiful peace pipe, which must have been in his family for generations. The pipe itself was made of the red stone, which the Chief explained was from a quarry several days north of the village. The red stone was highly prized and traded across the heartland of America. It had been shaped into an eagle's head and was quite magnificent. The stem was long and wooden with intricate patterns of bead work decorating it.

The Chief stood up, took several puffs on the pipe and offered its medicine to the six directions, North, South, East, West, above to the heavens and below to mother earth. He then held it over each of the kids welcoming them to this council and blessing them as fellow travelers on the journey to the Great Spirit. Then he handed it to the other elders who took puffs and passed it along until it had completed the circle. The Great Chief took a last puff and then carefully laid the pipe in front of him on a rabbit skin.

There was a long pause and then the Chief said in a warm voice, "Welcome, and thank you for helping Running Deer escape the currents of the Great River. Where are you from and what brings you to our land?"

Christy took a deep breath and then responded to the Chief's question. "We are not travelers of distance but of time. We are the descendants of those from across the great sea. We have come to share good will from our time and to learn of your wisdom." She then stopped, somewhat concerned that her comments might not be understood and perhaps she had said too much.

The Elders sat with eyes intent on Christy, Katy and John. There was silence for what seemed to the kids an eternity and then the Chief spoke.

"We have heard of the pale skinned people from across the sea from our brothers to the east and south. Some have even traded with a few of our people. Their impact on the tribes cannot be fully known at this time but I have seen in a dream that there will be sadness among the People unless we and they can learn to share the Earth's bounty." Again he paused, choosing his words carefully.

He continued, "Let me tell you about the People. Perhaps then you will understand. Guided by the Great Spirit who we call Wauconda, we came here long before anyone can remember. Wauconda, created all that there is, and placed us here as stewards of the land and its many plants and animals. We take from the earth only what we need and give back through our prayers, songs, dance and the beat of the sacred drum. We maintain the balance by being a point of communion between heaven and earth."

There was another long pause.

Then Katy asked, "Tell us about the prayers which the hunters say over their quarry. We saw one of the People saying a prayer over a large deer as we came into your village today."

The Chief smiled at Katy, for he knew that she had witnessed something special. He then said, "You have asked about one of the ways that the People maintain the balance. When we take from the earth we always thank the spirit of the animal for its sacrifice. The prayers reflect our gratitude to the Great Spirit and also are a promise that through the People the animal will become a part of something greater. The deer you saw will feed us and clothe us. We take only what we need and nothing is wasted. It is the way."

John, who couldn't wait to speak, quickly jumped in, "Can you tell us about the celebration tonight?"

"Gladly, my young friend," the Chief answered. "On full moons and other times as written in the movement of the stars and planets, we celebrate. The People from many villages join us for the more important occasions celebrating the season's hunt and harvest. We sing, chant, play the magic tones of the flute and beat the sacred drum while all dance in the perfect rhythm of earth and sky. Each song we sing celebrates the wonder of life. Wa Ta Ho Ta Ho, a song you will hear tonight, welcomes all to the Grand Council. Each dance thanks Wauconda for the Great Spirit's endless gifts. All are invited to share the sacred joy of the Grand Council, for all are one with the Great Spirit and a part of the bridge between above and below. With each step or stomp of the moccasin know that you are pushing the sacred energy into our great mother. She then responds by reflecting the love back out to all life in a great circle. It is an endless dance of giving and receiving, always in perfect balance."

"Wow," said John and then there was silence.

The Chief stood up as did the Elders, each giving a slight head nod of acknowledgement to the children, and left Long House.

"Come," said Running Deer. "We have much to do to prepare for Grand Council." And they followed Running deer out of the Long House.

Now that the Elders had officially welcomed the children, the People of the village treated them with a different energy, a respect as one of their own as opposed to being just a curiosity.

Running Deer made sign language signals to some of his friends as we passed. They quickly ran away, but soon returned with moccasins and dance bustles. A dance bustle is worn on the lower back of a dancer and looks like a round shield made of leather, beadwork and feathers. The central area is decorated by beadwork and feathers radiate out from there, forming a circle a few feet across. Smaller bustles are often worn on a dancers upper arms. The moccasins were very similar to those from the kids time, except with a soft deerskin sole. Christy, Katy and John were each given a pair of moccasins and a bustle for the lower back.

"Sweet," said John. Wow and sweet were John's favorite words and he often used them when all other expressions of amazement fell short.

"They are beautiful," said Christy and Katy. "They must have taken hours to make."

The kids thanked Running Deer and his friends over and over again. Running Deer and his friends were more than a little surprised at all the gratitude and beamed a huge smile, while blushing slightly at all the attention.

Grand Council was scheduled to begin at sunset. For Christy, Katy and John, who were overcome with excitement, sunset could not come fast enough. The village was buzzing as final preparations were made. Many others began to arrive from other villages and all were in their ceremonial dress. Feathers, bustles, elaborate beadwork on leather shirts and moccasins and headwear of feathers earned over the years by the wearer, commemorating some special achievement. It was a spectacle of color.

"Hurry," said Running Deer, "or we will miss the procession."

They ran to the outskirts of the village where all were lining up behind the Chief. Following behind him were other Chiefs and Elders from the visiting villages, and then the many dancers and celebrants.

Exactly at sunset the procession began with the beat of the great drum carried by two of the braves. The drum beat steadily as the procession solemnly moved towards the Council Ring. Boom, Boom, Boom, Boom; with each beat of the drum, another step was taken by the processors. Upon reaching the Council Ring, all circled the stone border and the drum was carefully placed on its stand in front of the Chief. There was silence as a young man began to sing:

Wa Ta Ho Ta Ho
Wa Ta Ho Ta Ho
Wa Ut Ta Ho Na We Tan Alo
Wa Ut Ta Ho Ta He Man Alo
Ma Yen Na We Zu Me Teth Lan E
Ma Yen Na We Zu Me Ta Na Le
Wa Ta Ho Ta Ho
Wa Ta Ho Ta Ho

This was an ancient song of the People, welcoming all to the Grand Council and imploring the Great Spirit to smile upon all.

Then, while everyone remained silent, a young man, walked to the center of the Council Ring with a leather deer skin bag of tools. He knelt before the unlit fire that had been carefully laid earlier in the day, and pulled a bow, drill and base from his bag. Running Deer whispered to Christy, Katy and John that the items in the bag were used to light the Council Fire using friction.

Taking the small wooden drill which was about 8 inches long and an inch in diameter, the young man wrapped the string of the bow around the drill. The string was made of animal sinew and was loose enough on the bow to wrap the drill one time firmly so that the backward and forward movement of the bow would spin the drill against the wood block used as a base. Back and forth he spun the drill into the base, until friction generated a red hot coal. The brave then carefully placed the coal within tinder prepared earlier, which was very dry, and with a little blowing the coal and tinder together would turn into a flame which would then light the Council fire. All this the fire-lighter accomplished flawlessly in about a minute. Within a short time the fire was blazing; it's light flickering and casting shadows in all directions.

As the young brave gathered his fire lighting equipment and walked from the center of the ring, many in the crowd began to whoop and holler in appreciation of a job well done.

Then the sound of the drum broke the silence, and the dances began. Several dances celebrated the hunt. The kids of the village often danced as buffalo or deer as the older braves stalked and chased them around the ring. All was done with great fun, but also great reverence.

These were followed by dances celebrating the maize harvest, dances invoking rain, dances involving boogey men which always got the attention of the young ones, and dances of the eagle and the hawk. Any activity or event that related to the survival and prosperity of the village had a dance associated with it.

I was somewhat disappointed that there weren't any dances which featured cats, but I wasn't about to leave the safety of my perch on top of Long House to correct the oversight. Thankfully, there weren't any dances about dogs either.

After several specific dances, all were invited to dance in the Council Ring. The drum beat began again, and almost immediately the Council Ring was filled with color and energy. It looked like one joyous free for all. Every dancer was showing his or her particular dance prowess while connecting with the Great Spirit, and simultaneously, with the People. It was chaos, but it was an ordered chaos. John had jumped up immediately when all were invited to enter the Council Ring. After some gentle persuasion from Running Deer, Christy and Katy also joined the growing crowd.

"There are two basic steps," Running Deer explained, barely audible over the noise of the dancing and the drum. "They are the single toe heel step and the double toe heel step. From these have evolved dozens of different steps like the cross over and the sty-u, many specific to individual dancers. But it is the spirit and intention of the dancer which creates the energy of the Grand Council and all dancers are welcome, no matter how proficient."

With that, Running Deer demonstrated the single toe heel and the double toe heel. Christy, Katy and John soon got the basics down and were dancing as if they were born to it. With each step it became easier, and more importantly, the kids became less self-conscious. They soon began to feel the energy and remembered the Chiefs words about sharing the energy of the dance with mother earth. Seeing each step as a gift to the earth, they soon lost themselves in the ceremony. In the intensity of the their new found exhilaration, they were more than startled when several village members swept them up into a line of dancers weaving in serpentine fashion around and across the Council Ring. Without warning the line left the Council Ring and weaved its way through the village. Always there was enjoyment, yet always there was reverence and solemnity.

In time the dance line rejoined their brothers and sisters in the Council Ring. Christy, Katy and John were enthralled. They danced until late in the evening, knowing that they were a part of something meaningful, something larger than just themselves, something sacred. They hoped it would never end. They danced on and on, and then at a point of utter exhaustion there was a loud final Boom of the drum head. It was over, for now. But they had felt the energy of Grand Council and knew it was in the people, the earth and the sky, radiating and returning in a great circle. And so it ever was.

The next morning the kids were awakened by a ray of sunlight streaming between a crack in the bark roof of the hut where they were sleeping. Their bustles and moccasins were neatly piled in a corner near the buffalo robes which had kept them warm in the night. With a sudden realization of where they were, they jumped up and ran outside. The village was already up cooking food, preparing animal skins, making arrows, all the things needed for the welfare of the village and the People.

I woke up before the sun, and had already consumed a tasty mouse treat, before anyone stirred.

Seeing the kids, Running Deer greeted them and asked how they slept. They all agreed that they had never slept so well.

"Thank you Running Deer," they said in unison. "Thank you for everything."

Blushing slightly, Running Deer responded. "It is I who should be thanking you. Remember, you pulled me from the river," he said betraying a slight smile.

"Time has flown by," said John, with Katy quickly agreeing. "It will be hard to leave today, but we promise to return soon."

"Leave," said Running Deer somewhat startled. "I guess I knew you would have to leave, but so soon?"

"Yes, but we will be back before you know it. In fact, we will be back, even if we have to turn back the hands of time," Christy said, while at the same time giving a quick wink to Katy and John.

"Good," said Running Deer. "Remember, you are members of the village now and friends for life. You will always be welcome."

"Well, I guess we should go. Short goodbyes, long friendships," she continued while fighting back a small tear.

Running Deer's face was full of a happy sadness. "Wait here," and he ran back to the hut the kids stayed in that night. Returning with Christy's backpack, he said, "Can't forget this." He gave each of his new friends a warm hug.

With some sadness, but also great joy, Christy, Katy and John waved to the village people who had gathering along the road to wish them safe travels. Then they turned and were on their way.

"Come on Kit," John called and I quickly followed.

Wow, what an amazing experience, they thought to themselves. Within a short time we were in sight of Big Hill. As we approached, the crystal began to glow, but at the top of the hill there was no sign of XJ, only the limestone cliff. We continued to approach the cliff, now becoming slightly concerned. But just as XJ had promised, the cave revealed itself when we were only a foot or so away. Above the door was the now familiar infinity symbol. With a considerable sigh of relief, the kids entered the cave. Of, course, I was never concerned, despite the constant flick of my tail giving me away.

We soon were greeted by the soft humming and pulsating light of the Time Machine. "Welcome back travelers. How was your .....," XJ began. But before he could finish, a distinct buzzing was heard. "My sensors detect something from this time period in you possession."

"I don't think so," said Christy. "We left the moccasins and dance bustles back at the hut in the village."

"You better check just to make sure," said XJ.

Opening up her back pack, Christy gasped. "There are three pairs of dance moccasins in here. Running Deer must have put them in here when he ran back to the hut to get my backpack."

"Can we keep them," implored John, "please?"

XJ sighed. "I wish you could, but sometimes the smallest thing can change your time line or the time line visited. Leave them here for now, but I may have an idea. Trust me."

With that, the kids climbed into the Time Machine and began the trip home. I was already comfortably perched on my jump seat. The craft began to hum and then flash with increasing frequency. The flashing became so rapid that it seemed to the human eye that it was a steady glow. The big screen flashed the seasons, but this time in a normal progression of Summer, Fall, Winter and Spring. And then, as quickly as it began, it stopped.

"We're here," said XJ.

"That was quick," said Katy. "I think I hear Bong-Bong."

"See you next time and don't forget to check the wall on your way out," said XJ.

"Thank you XJ," they said as they left. See you tomorrow." Climbing down from their trusty craft, Christy, Katy and John quickly ran over to the cliff wall to see what XJ might be referring to.

"Look," said John excitedly. "It's our whole trip drawn on the wall just like the other petroglyphs."

"There we are rescuing Running Deer, and there we are in the Long House meeting the Chief and Elders and there we are dancing," they each enthusiastically pointed out. I was also well represented in the petroglyphs and this gave my tail endless satisfaction as it flicked back and forth for almost a minute. I know that seems like a short time, but we cats can't show too much emotion.

Christy, Katy and John followed the pictographs from their trip to the very end and there by the picture of the Time Machine and related controls were three pairs of moccasins perfectly represented on the wall. Even though they couldn't take the moccasins home with them, XJ had preserved them for eternity. My kids smiled happily and my tail flicked with satisfaction.

Until next time…..